Harold Snipperpot's Best Disaster Ever

Copyright © 2019 by Beatrice Alemagna

English translation copyright © 2019 by Edward Gauvin

For information address HarperCollins Children's Books, a division of HarperCollins Publishers,

195 Broadway, New York, NY 10007.

www.harpercollinschildrens.com

Library of Congress Cataloging-in-Publication Data

Names: Alemagna, Beatrice, author, illustrator. | Gauvin, Edward, translator.
Title: Harold Snipperpot's best disaster ever / Beatrice Alemagna.
Description: First edition. | New York, NY : Harper, An Imprint of HarperCollinsPublishers, [2019]
| "English translation by Edward Gauvin"—Title page verso. | Summary: Lonely seven-year-old
Harold Phillip Snipperpot is excited when his parents, not known for their affection, throw him
a birthday party attended exclusively by animals, but things take a turn when his guests start
destroying the house, forcing Harold to try and save his party from calamity,
with surprising results.
Identifiers: LCCN 2017057325 | ISBN 9780062498823 (hardcover)
Subjects: | CYAC: Birthdays—Fiction. | Parties—Fiction. | Animals—Fiction.
Classification: LCC PZ7.A3744 Har 2019 | DDC [E]—dc23 LC record available at
https://lccn.loc.gov/2017057325

The artist used gouache, oil, collage, and wax pencils
to create the illustrations for this book.
Typography by Amy Ryan
18 19 20 21 22 SCP 10 9 8 7 6 5 4 3 2 1

First Edition

Harold Snipperpot's Best Disaster Ever

words and pictures by

BEATRICE ALEMAGNA

HARPER

An Imprint of HarperCollinsPublishers

Some days feel like complete disasters. You feel turned upside down, and it seems impossible that anything good could happen.

Well, let me tell you the whole story from the beginning.

It was one week before the disaster, and I was turning seven. More than anything, I, Harold Phillip Snipperpot, wanted a real birthday party. I had never had one because my parents hated parties.

If you want to know why, it's because they were very grumpy.

They never hugged or laughed. And forget about a kiss good night—they barely even talked.

So each year on my birthday, nothing happened.

But this year I felt extra sad. So sad that my parents got worried. So worried that they decided to do something about it.

"We'll call up Mr. Ponzio," my mom said.

Everyone in our neighborhood goes to Mr. Ponzio with their problems. That's what his job is—to solve people's problems. In very original ways.

"I don't have any kids to send over, but I've got another idea," Mr. Ponzio explained. "Don't worry one bit, Mrs. Snipperpot. This party will be absolutely extraordinary."

"But will it make our son happy?"

"Yes, of course it will," he said. "Trust me! You will never forget it."

So my parents agreed.

On the day of the party, our house looked great—
all decked out with ribbons, banners, and a
rainbow of balloons. When the doorbell rang,
I ran to answer it.

And, whoooa—we couldn't believe what we saw.

There were real animals, a line of them—winding all the way up the street to our front door.

We were flabbergasted.

The animals made their way into our house one by one. At first, everything was fine, and my parents almost seemed to be enjoying themselves.

But before too long, something changed.

The animals began behaving . . . like animals!
Large mammals, I now know, are born decorators.
They immediately moved the furniture around and
opened and wrecked every drawer.

A polar bear clawed the velvet
sofa while a small herd of sheep
and pigs gobbled up the stuffing
and ate each pillow.

A giraffe reached up and chomped the crystals right off our Art Deco chandelier (a family heirloom!), and that was when my father collapsed.

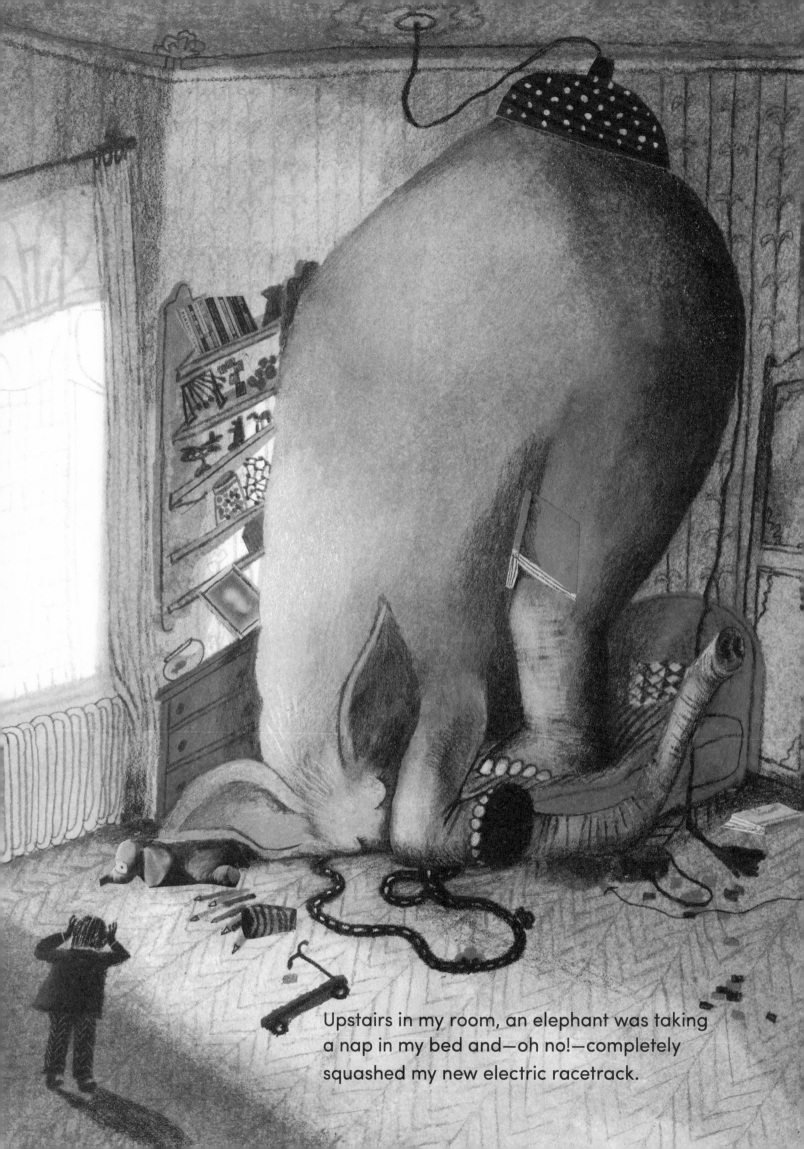

Upstairs in my room, an elephant was taking a nap in my bed and—oh no!—completely squashed my new electric racetrack.

Where was Mr. Ponzio? This was a mess!

Meanwhile, a medium-size flock of birds flew into the kitchen and performed a symphony—on my grandmother's china!

A family of turtles and their reptile friends demolished my father's library and gnawed an entire shelf of his rare-book collection.

A hippo found her way into the bathroom, ran a tub, and was soaking. All her pond pals followed—overflowing the tub and flooding the floor! My poor mom. She was too afraid to look.

Frolicking in my mother's closet were a seal, three monkeys, an armadillo, and others trying on her tulle skirts and her silk scarves—and tearing them to shreds. A goat was wearing her shoes!

Our house was destroyed, ruined, turned upside down. Worse yet, it was buried underneath a carpet of animal poo—every type—which really stank!

The party was *absolutely extraordinary*, all right!

Just then, a huge alligator flashed two rows
of sharp teeth at my parents, who, utterly
terrified, jumped into an old steamer trunk.

Oh no! The lid snapped shut and locked them inside.

I was trying to saw the lid off to free them when out of nowhere—

Mr. Ponzio appeared, waving a stick.

At the sight of the stick, the elephant panicked and stampeded toward the door. I had just enough time to grab its ears, and the rest of the animals followed us.

There I was, on an elephant, galloping through town, while my parents screamed like crazy from inside a steamer trunk on top of a rhino! What a disaster!

But when I looked around, it all suddenly seemed funny. Crowds of people snapped photos in the streets, adding even more commotion and chaos. And I was there, at the front of the line, when I had the greatest idea.

I, Harold Phillip Snipperpot, took charge and led the entire parade toward the fountain, where each animal stopped and took a sip of water—including the rhino, who dropped the steamer trunk, which fell to the ground and finally opened.

My parents climbed out, looking very relieved, and in front of everyone—I could hardly believe it—gave each other a big kiss. A giant passionate one, just like in a movie.

And then they gave one to me!

Seeing those kisses, the chameleons displayed their prettiest colors, which reflected in the water and lit up the entire park. Children from all over the neighborhood ran to see.

Some climbed the giraffe's neck, while others sat atop the alligator's back, and others gave the lion a new hairdo.

As for me? My mom swept me up in the air as I laughed and laughed.